Tweak Tweak

by EVE BUNTING

Illustrated by SERGIO RUZZIER

CLARION BOOKS

HOUGHTON MIFFLIN HARCOURT

Boston | New York | 2011

Clarion Books
215 Park Avenue South, New York, New York 10003
Text copyright © 2011 by Edward D. Bunting and Anne E. Bunting Family Trust
Illustrations copyright © 2011 by Sergio Ruzzier

The illustrations were executed in pen and ink and watercolors on paper.
The text was set in Aged Book.

For information about permission to reproduce selections from this book,
write to Permissions, Houghton Mifflin Harcourt Publishing Company,
215 Park Avenue South, New York, New York 10003.

Clarion Books is an imprint of Houghton Mifflin Harcourt Publishing Company.

www.hmhbooks.com

Library of Congress Cataloging-in-Publication Data is available.

LCCN: 2010024651
ISBN 978-0-618-99851-7

Manufactured in China
LEO 10 9 8 7 6 5 4 3 2 1
4500269754

To my five granddaughters, Dana, Anna, Tory, Erin, and Keelin,
with love — E.B.

To Elsa — S.R.

"Hold on to my tail, Little Elephant," Mama Elephant said. "Today we are going for a walk. If you want to ask me a question, tweak twice."

TWEAK, TWEAK!

"Yes, my little elephant?"

"Mama? What is that?"

6

"That is a frog."

"What is he doing?"

"He's jumping."

"Can I jump?"

8

"No, because you are not a frog. You are a little elephant. But you can stomp your foot and make a big sound."

STOMP, STOMP!

"Like that, Mama?"

"Just like that, my little elephant."

And on they went.

TWEAK,
TWEAK!

"Mama? What is that?"

"That is a monkey up in the acacia tree."

"Can I climb up in the acacia tree?"

"No, because you are not a monkey.
You are a little elephant. But you
can rub your back against the acacia
tree and scratch, scratch."

SCRATCH
SCRATCH

"Did that feel good, my little elephant?"

"Yes, Mama."

And on they went.

TWEAK,
TWEAK!

"Mama? What is that swimming in the river?"

"That is a crocodile."

"Can I go swimming in the river?"

"In another river, another time. But now you can pull up some river water in your trunk and spray it over yourself."

WHOOSH

WHOOSH

"Did that feel good, my little elephant?"

"Very good, Mama."

And on they went.

TWEAK,
TWEAK!

"Mama? What is that?"

"That is a beautiful butterfly flying high in the sky."

"Can I fly high in the sky?"

"No, because you are not a butterfly. You are a little elephant. But you can wave your ears back and forth, back and forth, like big butterfly wings."

SWISH
SWISH

SWISH
SWISH

"Did that feel good, my little elephant?"

"Very, very good, Mama."

And on they went.

TWEAK,
TWEAK!

"Mama? Who is that singing?"
"That is a songbird singing in the fig tree."

"No, because you are not a bird.
You are a little elephant. But you
can trumpet—like this. *RO-OAR!*
Try it!"

RO

...OAR!

"Like that, Mama?"

"Yes, just like that, my little elephant."

And on they went.

TWEAK,
TWEAK!

"Yes, my little elephant?"

"Mama, what else can a little elephant do?"

"A little elephant can walk through the jungle and across the grasslands holding her mother's tail. She can ask questions and learn. She can grow to be a big, strong, smart, beautiful elephant."

"Like you, Mama?"

"Yes. Just like me."

Tweak, tweak!

"Mama? Can we go home now?"

"Yes, my little elephant."

Tweak, tweak!

"Do you know the way back, my little elephant?"

"Yes, Mama. I remember."

And Little Elephant led Mama

past the fig tree where the bird sang,

past the place where the butterfly flew,

past the river where the crocodile swam,

past the acacia tree where the monkey climbed,

past the place where the frog jumped,

and all the way home.